HUGO AND ODDSOCK

TONY ROSS

Follett Publishing Company ✐ **Chicago**

Hugo the lardermouse looked longingly out of the window at the falling snowflakes.

"You *know* you can't go out and play in snow more than three inches deep!" squeaked Mama Lardermouse. "You'd disappear! Why don't you make a sock horse like I used to make when I was a mouselet?"

Hugo's ears twitched with interest. "What's a sock horse?" he said.

"If I can't play outside, what can I do?"

When Mama had climbed down from the high shelf, she began to tell Hugo of the wonderful sock horses she used to make years ago, when she lived with Uncle Townmouse. Hugo listened, whiskers quivering, until at last the time came for Mama to go shopping.

As she plodded away on her snow stilts, Hugo could only think of one thing . . . how to make a sock horse.

"G'morning Mrs. Lardermouse, cold enough to crack whiskers!"

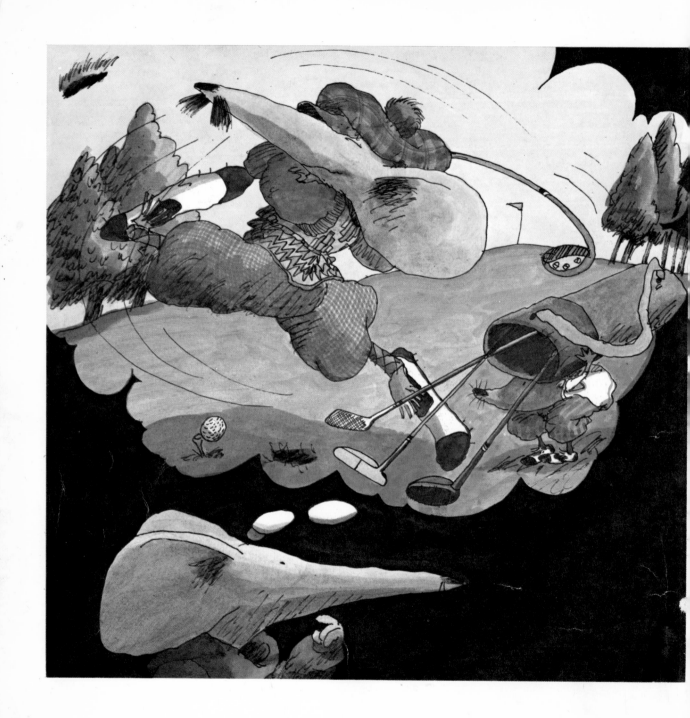

"I wonder IF?"

There was only one problem—lardermice don't wear socks.

Hugo sat down to think, and suddenly he thought of Uncle Townmouse. Uncle Townmouse had had a good job in the Tax Office, and he used to play golf.

Hugo bounded up to the attic and rummaged about in the box where some of Uncle Townmouse's old things were kept. Sure enough, he found what he was looking for . . . a beautiful, brown check golf-sock!

Hugo quickly found the other things he needed, and he started to make his sock horse.

First, he stuffed the sock with some old rags, pushing them down tightly.

Then he pulled the sock onto the end of a short pole, tying it firmly with some thick wool.

Two ears were cut from some stiff cloth. These were folded over and stitched on the place where ears should be. Two large white buttons were put on too, while Hugo had some cotton in his needle. These made splendid eyes.

As Hugo had lots of yellow wool, he made eight bunches, like tassels, and stitched them onto the sock for a mane. The sock horse looked more horse than sock now! Lengths of wool had to be plaited to make the reins. That was quite difficult, and took a long time, but Hugo managed it. He stitched two more buttons onto his horse and looped the reins onto them.
Finished!

"I'll call him ODDSOCK," thought Hugo.

"Chaaaaaaaaaaaaaaaaaaaaaaaaaaaaaarge!"

Almost at once, Hugo and Oddsock became the best of friends. Wearing a paper hat, and his trusty sword, the lardermouse waged fearsome battles with the living-room furniture, knocking down battalions of small tables, and regiments of ornaments. When Mama returned with her shopping, she was horrified to see the battlefield, and Fieldmarshal Hugo was packed off to bed without any supper. Oddsock, of course, went too!

Oddsock was put to bed by the toy chest, and Hugo fell asleep dreaming of tomorrow's battles.

A sudden noise awakened the mouse, who was astounded to see Oddsock crashing around the bedroom with a life all of his own. Hugo leaped out of bed, and just managed to grab the trailing rein as his horse made a sudden dart for the open window. Still gasping with amazement, the little mouse was pulled out into the dark night.

"Whhhhhhhhhhoooooooooaaaa!"

Oddsock gathered speed and surged into the sky like a rocket. Hugo clung on for dear life, gasping for breath. Soon the snow clouds were left far below, as Oddsock went up, and up, and up. Hugo began to take note of his surroundings, and got his second shock of the evening. He thought they were heading toward the moon, but, as they drew nearer to the shiny white circle, Hugo saw that it wasn't the moon at all. It was a hole in the night, and Oddsock was heading right through!

"Hellllllllllllllllllllllp . . . !"

"I'm Woollie, and I'm Willie."

Once through the hole in the night, Hugo saw a new world open up. Oddsock glided to earth in a huge, empty park surrounded by strange trees and towering buildings. As Hugo climbed off Oddsock's back, two funny little men trotted over. They seemed to be expecting the sock horse.

"Welcome to Lostsockland," they said at once, their voices mixing together like choir voices. "I'm Woollie, and I'm Willie. Come, we've work to do!"

The little twins trotted away, followed by Oddsock, followed in turn by a very bewildered pink lardermouse.

"Hang on, we'll be there in no time!"

The pair of sock twins led the way to a coach made from a gray schoolsock and pulled by a team of snow-white horses made from tennis socks. Once Hugo and Oddsock were settled, they all galloped away across rich countryside. Flocks of socks flew overhead, and from time to time Hugo glimpsed weird animals made from socks or long stockings.

The twins halted by one of the towering buildings and without a word showed the travellers inside.

"*Red pins are right socks, yellow ones left socks.*"

In a small laboratory at the top of the building, Woollie (or maybe Willie) told Hugo all about Lostsockland.

"You see, mouse, socks are always getting lost, or parted from each other, and when they do, they find their way here, and we make pairs out of them again. Socks can only be happy in pairs. That's why your Oddsock wanted to escape. My brother is looking in his book to find a friend for Oddsock." The other twin called out a number, and everybody turned to a map on the wall.

"That's where we must go!" said the first twin.

Another mad ride followed. The coach halted in a green field and Oddsock sprang down.

Another sock horse, just like Oddsock, trotted across the grass. The pair of lost socks nuzzled each other happily.

"Ahh! . . . " sighed the twins together.

"Hmm," thought Hugo, "I wonder if that could be a brown check golf-sock horse Mama made, all those years ago?" Somehow, he *knew* it was.

As Oddsock pranced away, Hugo imagined he heard a muffled "Thank you."

"Don't they make a fine pair, Woollie?"

Just as Hugo was beginning to worry about how he was going to get home without his horse, Willie (or it may have been Woollie) took his hand.

"Job's over now," he said abruptly. "Time we got you home."

He sang some strange words, and Hugo was snatched head over tail into the air. It was dark now, and he was spinning toward the hole in the night. On the other side it was dawn in his world. Below him, Oddsock was lost in herds of happy sock horses.

" . . . I hope I'm DREAMING!"

Hugo opened his eyes in his own little bedroom. "It must have all been a silly dream," he murmured, looking to where he had left Oddsock the night before. But Oddsock was not there. Hugo pulled his jersey over his pajamas and staggered downstairs, feeling strangely tired, as if he had been up all night.

Mama was in the kitchen making breakfast. She looked at Hugo and held up an odd sock.

"I can't think where socks get to when they get lost, can you?"

Hugo had a pretty good idea.

"Why do we always lose one sock, never TWO?"